The Pirate and the Pong Family

All At Sea

Written by Michaela Morgan
Illustrated by Martin Chatterton

D1632709

Chapter 1
Adventure!

Captain Kev was a happy, friendly pirate. He wasn't fierce at all. He had a fine parrot who was his *best* friend, and he now had other good friends too – the Potters. Captain Kev sang all day long.

Oh, a life at sea is the life for me, With the Potter family-eeee!

The Potters were once a very tidy and sensible family, but since they have been friends with Captain Kev they have become more and more piratical.

Captain Kev and the Potters were now sailing the Seven Seas. They loved the wide, blue sky and the deep, blue sea. They loved the salty sea air and the sense of adventure. And of course, they loved to sing.

"Shiver me timbers!" said Captain Kev. (This is how pirates say, "OH NOOOOOOOOOOOOOO!") "It's a pirate ship!" he explained. "Not all pirates are as nice as me!"

Trouble ahoy!

Chapter 2
Trouble!

Captain Kev was right. In no time at all, four fierce pirates and their parrot had clambered aboard Captain Kev's ship. They started to take whatever they wanted.

Pieces of eight! Nice fruit cake!

Charts and maps!

Hammocks for naps!

Comfy chair! Teddy bear!

Captain Kev bellowed, "Be off with ye!" Mum muttered and Gran tut-tutted. The baby HOWLED as his toys were stuffed in a sack …

… but Dad stood up and coughed politely.

Ahem!

He was holding a booklet called *The Pirate Code* and he read it out loud:

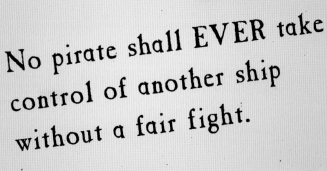

No pirate shall EVER take control of another ship without a fair fight.

"No problem!" said Bad Boris. "We'll fight you for the ship!"

Ooo-aaarrrr!

Chapter 3
Fight!

This is my best fighter, Red-Faced Ron. He'll fight any one of you!

Gran stood up. "*I'll* sort him out!" she challenged. She went right up to Red-Faced Ron. "Now, dear," she said, "why do they call you Red-Faced Ron?"

"Because I'm red with angry blood," he snarled. "I'm filled with fury. I'm like a volcano about to erupt. I'm …"

"Are you sure you haven't just been in the sun too long?" interrupted Gran. She examined him.

parched head

sore shoulder

chapped cheeks

blistered feet

"That looks very sore," said Gran.
"Try a spot of this cream."

"Aaaah," sighed Ron.
"That's soooo much better!"

"You need a hat to protect you from the sun," said Gran. "Come and choose one."

Red-Faced Ron sat down with Gran. They started chatting and trying on hats, just like old friends.

The next pirate wanting to fight was Quick Slick Old Nick, the fastest sword-fighter on the Seven Seas (or so *he* said). Billy stood up and drew his wooden sword. Quick Slick laughed, but this is how the fight went:

Billy was light on his feet. So was Lilly. They ran rings round Quick Slick Old Nick.

Then the parrots joined in the fight.
"Sticky beak!" Captain Kev's parrot squawked.
"Smelly feet!" replied Quick Slick's bird.

Up they went until ...

They hit the deck in a flurry of feathers. They saw stars and then ... hearts!

"My name's Jack," wooed Captain Kev's parrot.

"I'm Jill!" cooed Quick Slick Old Nick's parrot.

Aaaah, lovebirds!

Bad Boris was not giving up. "Here's my secret weapon!" he said. "Let me introduce ... Stinky O'Skunk. No one can beat 'im! No one can even come close."

"I can beat that!" Mum boasted ... and with a flourish, she whipped off Baby's nappy.

"Phew-ew-weeeeeee! You win!" said the pirates. "Nothing is worse than THAT!"

Chapter 4
Mates!

Bad Boris slumped. He was beaten. He looked ready to cry.

"Now, dear," said Gran, "why do you go around trying to take other people's boats and stuff?"

Bad Boris sobbed. "Life be truly terrible aboard our ship. There be no cosy comforts. No hearty meals. No jolly sing-songs. *You've* got a shiny, ship-shape ship and jolly good company. All we've got is beetles and rats … and even the rats are leaving."

"Oo-ar," said the sympathetic Potters.

"Then I say ye are all mighty welcome to join us," said Captain Kev. "There be plenty of room."

"And plenty of food!" said Mum.

"And we can all look for treasure together!" shouted Lilly and Billy.

"We can help organise your ship," said Gran. "It will soon be comfy and ship-shape, or my name isn't Granny Potter!"

"Which it is," Captain Kev explained.

The crew from the old pirate ship thought about it ... but not for long. With one voice, they shouted:

"Yes!"

... and "please," they added.

"Yippeee!!"

... and "thank you," they added. They were already starting to become nice, tidy, polite pirates.

That evening under the stars they all ate a good meal together, told tall tales and joined in the family song.

We're rough, tough pirates and we sail the Seven Seas,
We're rough, tough pirates and we've all got scabby knees,
We're rough, tough pirates and we do just what we please,
And we're going to have adventures,
And we're going to have adventures,
Just you wait and seeeeee!